LITTLE BOOK OF
LATIN AMERICAN
FOLKTALES

EDITED BY
CARMEN DIANA DEARDEN

TRANSLATED BY
Susana Wald and Beatriz Zeller

A Groundwood Book

Douglas & McIntyre Toronto Vancouver Berkeley

Copyright © 2003 by Ediciones Ekaré
Translation copyright © 2003 by Groundwood Books Ltd.
Simultaneously published in Spanish as *Libro de oro de los abuelos*
by Ediciones Ekaré, Caracas.

Groundwood Books / Douglas & McIntyre
720 Bathurst Street, Suite 500, Toronto, Ontario M5S 2R4

Distributed in the USA by Publishers Group West
1700 Fourth Street, Berkeley, CA 94710

We acknowledge for their financial support of our publishing program the Canada
Council for the Arts, the Ontario Arts Council and the Government of Canada
through the Book Publishing Industry Development Program (BPIDP).

National Library of Canada Cataloguing in Publication
Little book of Latin American folktales / edited by Carmen Diana Dearden;
translated by Susana Wald and Beatriz Zeller.
Translation of: Libro de oro de los abuelos.
ISBN 0-88899-543-1
1. Latin Americans–Folklore. 2. Tales–Latin America.
I. Dearden, Carmen Diana II. Wald, Susana III. Zeller, Beatriz
IV. Title.
PZ8.1.L58 2002   j398.2'098   C2002-903768-9

Library of Congress Control Number: 2002110621

Printed and bound in China

STORIES RETOLD BY
PILAR ALMOINA DE CARRERA
PASCUALA CORONA
RAFAEL OLIVARES FIGUEROA
CARMEN HENY
RAFAEL RIVERO ORAMAS
MARGOT SILVA PÉREZ

WITH PICTURES BY
MARÍA FERNANDA OLIVER
HEINZ ROSE
IRENE SAVINO

TABLE OF CONTENTS

INTRODUCTION

Folktales are enjoyable to listen to and tell because they express people's deepest desires, dreams, hopes and idio-syncrasies. These are stories spun over centuries, and they hold the integrity, depth of meaning and mystery that touch each of us intimately. They have the ability to cut across social barriers and geographic borders.

When stories travel, they change. New storytellers draw on elements of their own culture, place and time to adapt tales to their own worlds. Thus traditional European tales made their way to Latin America, where they were told over and over again, and in the retelling they were transformed, as old elements combined with the new. They became part of the *Criollo* (Creole) culture – the mestizo culture of the Europeans transformed by their contact with the New World. It is a culture that has evolved since the arrival of the Spaniards in North America.

The ten stories in this anthology are Spanish American versions of tales from many parts of the world, passed from generation to generation and carried over into Latin

American and Venezuelan lore. The retellings here are by great storytellers who have collected, retold and infused these stories with *Criollo* elements.

The authors of this anthology (whose biographies are found at the end of the book) range from folklorists to simple storytellers. They all valued highly their *Criollo* culture and its roots, and they specifically looked for local tales at a time when pride in and curiosity about the *Criollo* culture was emerging, and Europe was no longer the only point of cultural reference that mattered. This anthology brings alive the voices of those who are now the elders of this literary heritage. Through their voices children today will find great pleasure in tales that reflect both the Old and the New Worlds that combine to make up Latin America.

All of these stories have one thing in common – a kind of humor native to Spanish America. It is particularly reflected in the sparkle that imbues the language of the people who tell these stories as part of their daily lives, as part of the blanket they spread over their children every night at bedtime – because, as Lewis Carroll said, Stories are gifts of love.

Carmen Diana Dearden

Notes to the Stories

•**Juan Cenizo** is the oft-told story of the younger brother who does things better than his older brothers. It is almost identical in structure to "The Flying Boat," a Russian folktale featuring the fast-running man, the big eater, the big drinker and the outstanding hunter.

•**The Girl and the Fish** features a fish that comes out of the water every time someone calls it, a motif not unlike that of "The Fisherman and His Wife," except that it is developed in an entirely different manner. The Venezuelan story deals not with excessive greed but with a first love thwarted by the parents. Some folktale experts claim that the story has its roots in Africa.

•**Little Chitlings** is a variation on the motif of the girl who is good and evil and who is either rewarded or punished for her behavior. In the story collected by the Brothers Grimm, the evil girl has toads and snakes coming out of her mouth; in the Venezuelan story, she has grown a wattle on her forehead.

•A version of **Whiteflower** exists in Spain. The title is the same and it is very similar to the one included here. In both instances the heroine uses her magic powers with great self-confidence in order to help the man she likes pass the tests that her father sets for him.

•**Crooked Foot the Dwarf** is none other than the small but courageous tailor who fools the giant with the cunning and charm of Pedro Rimales.

•In **The Basil Pot** we find the woman who competes with the king's inventiveness and succeeds in conquering him.

•**María Tolete** is a tropical version of "Cinderella," where the fairy godmother is missing entirely, but the passionate motif of the stranger at the ball is preserved.

•**The Griffin** is related to the German tale by the same name, as well as to "The Devil's Three Hairs," where the hero must surmount the difficult task of taking three hairs from the devil, or three feathers from the Griffin, in order to win the king's daughter's hand in marriage.

•**Ocelot, Jaguar and Lion** is a Venezuelan version of "Hansel and Gretel," where a one-eyed old woman frying meat has replaced the gingerbread house.

•In Spain there is a story similar to **The Talking Bird, the Singing Tree and the Fountain of Gold**, with the age-old motif of children who are thrown into the river, rescued by peasants and reunited with their father the king, who has kept the queen imprisoned for years. In this version it is the youngest sister who succeeds in saving her brothers. This story has convinced many girls of the power women hold.

Juan Cenizo

RETOLD BY
PILAR ALMOINA DE CARRERA
ILLUSTRATED BY
IRENE SAVINO

There once was a lady who had three sons. Two of them were very bright, but the third, whose name was Juan Cenizo, had a reputation for being a little slow.

There was also in those days a king who sent out word that whoever built him a ship capable of sailing on both water and land would win the right to marry his daughter.

When he heard this, the oldest of the three brothers said, "I am going to build the ship and marry the princess."

He asked his mother to prepare his gear and food he would need for the journey. His mother made a delicious big sandwich and said goodbye at the door of their house. And so the oldest of the

three brothers went to the mountain to cut down the trees he would need to build the boat. However, when he was about to cross the river, he met a woman with a child in her arms.

"Help me and the boy to cross the river," she asked.

"It wasn't me who told you to have the child," the young man answered. And he crossed the river by himself without looking back.

When he got to the mountain he felled a tree. He had just started to chop it into pieces when an old man came by.

"Do you have anything to eat, young man?" he asked.

"Yes, I have a sandwich, but it is for me alone," said the bright young man.

"And what are you planning to make with that tree trunk?"

"Spinning tops and spoons," the young man answered.

"That's exactly what you'll get out of that wood," said the old man.

The young man spent the whole day trying to

build a boat, but as soon as the ax touched the wood, it turned into spinning tops and spoons. Finally he got tired of the useless effort and went back home.

That was when the second of the clever brothers announced that he was going to marry the princess, because he was going to succeed in building the ship. He asked his mother to prepare his gear and food for his journey to the mountain. She baked him a tasty sponge cake.

Brother number two started on his way and, as he began to cross the river, he ran into the same woman with the child.

"Help me and the boy to cross the river," said the woman. But the young man gave the same answer as his older brother.

"It wasn't me who told you to have the child." And he crossed the river without helping her.

He came to the mountain to cut the trees. He cut down the first one and just at that moment, the same old man appeared.

"Do you have anything to eat, young man?" he asked.

"Yes, some sponge cake, but it's all for me."

"And what are you planning to do with that tree trunk?"

"Spinning tops and spoons."

To which the old man answered, "And that's exactly what you'll get out of that wood."

The old man disappeared while the second of the brothers began to cut up the tree. But every time the ax touched the wood, only spinning tops and spoons came out. The young man soon tired of this and went back home.

Then Juan Cenizo, the brother whom people called a fool, said that he would marry the king's daughter, as he was the one who would build a boat that could sail on both water and land. And he asked his mother to prepare his gear and food for his journey to the mountain.

"But if your clever brothers could not do it, how do you, the fool, expect to accomplish this?" asked his mother.

"Well, I'm going to go, anyway," said Juan Cenizo. His mother went off to prepare the gear and the food. All she had left, however, was a cock, which is what she cooked for him.

He left cheerfully the next day. As he was getting ready to cross the river, he ran into the woman with the child in arms.

"Help me across with the child," she said.

Juan Cenizo carefully held the child and took him to the other side of the river. He then helped the woman across and said goodbye.

He continued on his way up the mountain and, when he found a tall and straight tree, he began to cut it down. That is when the little old man appeared.

"Do you have anything to eat, young man?" he asked.

"Yes, I have a cock my mother prepared for me. We can share it," Juan Cenizo answered.

When they had finished eating, the little old man told Juan to keep on working and disappeared. No sooner had Juan Cenizo grabbed hold of the ax and turned to the tree in order to chop it down, than he saw that the boat had already been built. Delighted, he climbed in and started toward the king's palace.

He was sailing along in the middle of the forest when he met a man carrying a sack of corn.

"Give me a ride," said the man.

"Who are you?" asked Juan Cenizo.

"I am Florín Floridor, the Great Eater."

To prove the point, he leaned down and in one bite ate the whole sack of toasted corn.

"Come along with me," said Juan Cenizo, and Florín Floridor climbed into the boat.

They kept sailing through the forest and a little while later they met another man who was drinking water from the river.

Juan Cenizo stopped the boat and asked, "Who are you?"

"I am Amín Amador, the Great Drinker."

At that, he leaned down and swallowed the whole river in one gulp. He then climbed into the boat and they continued on their way to the king's palace.

A little while later they came upon a man hunting birds with a sling.

Juan Cenizo stopped the boat and asked, "Who are you?"

"I am Niquín Nicanor, the Great Hunter."

He immediately took aim with his sling and killed a bird that was flying three hundred leagues away. He then climbed into the boat and away they sailed through the woods.

Soon they ran into a man who was blowing out of one of his nostrils.

"Who are you?" asked Juan Cenizo.

"I am Sofín Sofanor, the Great Blower."

And he blew from one of his nostrils and all the trees of the mountain in front of them came crashing down.

"Come with me," said Juan, and the man climbed into the boat.

They continued to sail on land and on water until they arrived at the king's palace.

Juan Cenizo told the guards that he had brought the boat the king had asked for and the guards let them through.

The king was amazed to see the beautiful boat,

and he told the princess that she had to marry Juan Cenizo. But no sooner did the princess look at him than she said she would never marry such a fool, and she convinced the king to test Juan Cenizo. Juan agreed, but on the condition that one of his friends could accompany him.

The princess gave orders to fill one room in the palace with food. Juan Cenizo was to eat it all in one day.

Juan asked Florín Floridor to come with him, and the guards locked them in the room. In a one, two, three, Florín Floridor, the Great Eater, had eaten all the food.

Furious, the princess then gave orders to fill the room with drink.

"You will now drink all the drinks that are in there," she said.

This time Juan asked Amín Amador to accompany him. The guards locked them in the room and in the time it takes a rooster to crow, Amín Amador, the Great Drinker, had drunk it all until not a drop was left.

The princess angrily told Juan Cenizo that she would stand on the other side of the palace's pond and raise her hand. With a single shot, Juan was to shoot off the precious stone on her ring. That was when Juan asked Niquín Nicanor to go with him. The guards locked them in a room and from the window, Niquín Nicanor, the Great Hunter, aimed at the ring. With a single slingshot he removed the stone from her ring before the princess even realized what had happened.

Now the princess was really angry. She said there was no way she would marry Juan Cenizo. But the king insisted because Juan had successfully completed the three tests and he had to keep his promise.

The princess then invented a fourth test.

She wanted Juan to bring water back from the farthest spring in the kingdom before the return of the carrier pigeon she was about to let loose. Juan said this was fine, but he asked for a crystal glass and said that Sofín Sofanor would accompany him. They locked them in a room. From inside the tower of the castle, the princess let loose the pigeon. That was when Sofín Sofanor, the Great Blower, blew through one of his nostrils with all the strength and gentleness he could muster. The air carried away the crystal glass until it reached the most distant spring and flew back filled with clear and fresh water right into the hands of the princess, before the pigeon arrived.

The king told his daughter, "Now you do have to marry him."

And so it was.

However, on the very day of the wedding the princess said, "Since you are capable of doing so many strange and difficult things, why don't you change that stupid face of yours?"

"Fine," said Juan, and he changed his own face.

The princess was delighted with Juan's new face, but now she wanted something else. She asked him to build her a better palace than the king's.

The next morning her wish was realized. Juan Cenizo and the princess found themselves in a beautiful palace. Upon seeing this, the guards went to tell the king that there was a better palace across from his.

"Tell the fool to come here," the king ordered.

The guards ran to give Juan Cenizo the message. He had the guards tell the king that his palace was exactly the same distance from the king's as the king's was from his, and that the king should therefore come to him.

The king went over to Juan Cenizo's palace, but upon seeing that the fool was no longer a fool, he took off his crown and placed it on Juan's head.

THE GIRL AND THE FISH

RETOLD BY
PILAR ALMOINA DE CARRERA
ILLUSTRATED BY
HEINZ ROSE

There were two children, a girl and a boy, who lived with their parents in a hut. Every day the children went to the hills to collect the firewood that was needed in the house.

One day there was a very heavy downpour, but once the rain had finally stopped, the children went to the hills as they always had. While they were there, the girl discovered a small pond with a little fish swimming in it. She gazed at it while her brother finished picking up wood.

After awhile the girl sang a little song to the fish:

Swordfish, siren, boom bo bish
Are you my friend, siren, swordfish?

She sang again and the fish came out of the water and said,

Cay yoon, cay yoon, here I am.

"What are you doing, sister?" asked her brother.
"I am looking at the little fish I will marry."

The brother and sister went back home but said nothing to their parents.

The next day they went out for firewood again. The girl took bread crumbs to the fish and sang the same song she had sung the day before. And the fish came out of the water again.

So the days passed, and the girl kept visiting the fish.

In time, the pond became bigger and deeper and the little fish grew into a huge one, and the girl turned into a beautiful young woman.

Her parents started to get angry because she

always wanted to go for firewood, and she took a long time coming back. They began to question her brother, until he could no longer keep the secret to himself. He told them that a huge fish spoke to his sister when she sang a song.

The next day, when the brother and sister went out for firewood, the parents secretly followed. They saw how the fish came out of the water, spellbound by the song of the young woman.

After the young woman left, her parents approached the pond and the father sang,

Swordfish, siren, boom bo bish
Are you my friend, siren, swordfish?

The fish, upon hearing that booming voice, sank deeper into the water.

Then the mother, imitating her daughter's voice, sang,

Swordfish, siren, boom bo bish
Are you my friend, siren, swordfish?

The fish, thinking that the young woman was calling him, came right out of the water and sang,

Cay yoon, cay yoon, here I am.

The father quickly gave it a blow and stunned it. Then they took the fish out of the pond and carried it to the hut, where they cleaned it and prepared it for the evening meal. They hid its scales in the daughter's trunk.

When the brother and sister came home, the mother laid out the meal. The girl said that she wasn't hungry and went to her room. When she opened the trunk and saw the scales, she understood what had happened. Terrible pain filled her heart over the death of the fish. She ran to the pond and saw that it had dried up. She left the scales where the pond had been and sat down crying inconsolably.

When the parents saw that their daughter was gone, they went to the pond looking for her, but all they could find were a few strands of her hair growing from the ground. They pulled at them with all their might and called her name, but there was no answer.

The girl had disappeared, following the memory of her beloved fish.

LITTLE CHITLINGS

RETOLD BY
MARGOT SILVA PÉREZ
ILLUSTRATED BY
MARÍA FERNANDA OLIVER

There was once a young girl who had to stay at home with her stepmother and stepsister when her father went away on a long journey. As soon as he was gone, the stepmother and stepsister began to treat her badly.

One day they sent her to clean chitlings to make mondongo stew. The girl went to the river to wash the chitlings and as she was going about her work, a sardine came up, grabbed the tips of the chitlings and took them away. Frightened, the girl ran along the shore of the river, shouting, "Little sardine, little sardine, give me back the chitlings!"

But the sardine swam so fast that it almost flew. The girl was unable to catch up with it and, running and running behind it, she ended up far from home.

When she finally decided it was time to go back (though without the chitlings), she realized she was hopelessly lost. She looked this way and that but saw only a narrow path that led her to a small blue house. At the door was a little old blind man sitting in a big chair.

He heard the girl's steps approaching and said, "I am very thirsty. Can you bring me a glass of water?"

"Yes," said the girl, and she went into the house.

While she was in the kitchen she decided to cook the little old man some breakfast, so she made cornmeal rolls and coffee with a dash of milk. The little old man ate everything. The girl washed him, combed his hair and made him look handsome. Then she said that she had to go home.

"It is not time yet," the little old man answered. From the house, she could hear a baby crying. "The baby is hungry. Could you take care of him?"

The girl went into the house and saw the child in his crib, crying and crying.

She took him in her arms, bathed him, made him soup and put him to sleep.

"It is time for me to go," said the girl. "Goodbye."

"No, it is not time yet, girl," said the little old man. As he spoke, a great racket could be heard in the chicken coop.

"What is happening to those chickens? Have they gone crazy?" the girl asked.

"They are hungry and thirsty," said the man.

The girl then went for water and corn and the chickens calmed down.

"Now I must leave," she said.

"It is not time yet," said the little old man, and she could hear a dog moaning with hunger.

The girl fed it, petted it and said goodbye to the little old man, but he said again, "It is not time yet," and she could hear the cat meowing.

She gave it milk in a bowl, stroked its back until it began to purr and again said goodbye.

"It is not yet time to leave," said the little old man once more, as a voice yelling from inside the house was heard. "The parrot is behind the door. He's starving, poor little parrot!"

The girl found the parrot behind the door and fed it, too.

"*Now* it is time to leave," said the little old man, and the girl finally said goodbye.

She was walking down the path when she noticed that the garden was all dried up, the flowers wilting under the fierce sun.

"I can't leave these flowers like this," she thought, and she went back to water them. She was watering the plants when she heard steps and hid behind some bushes, frightened.

"Who could it be?" she thought.

Standing there were seven tall, beautiful ladies. One of them approached the little old man and asked, "Grandpa, who made you look so handsome?"

"A girl that came here," answered the man.

"May she be the most beautiful girl in the town," the lady said.

The second lady went into the house and saw the sleeping baby.

"Who looked after my baby, Grandpa?" she asked.

"A girl that came here," answered the grandfather.

"Then that girl must have a star on her forehead," said the second lady.

The third lady found the chickens happily running, cackling and laying eggs.

"Who fed my chickens with water and corn, Grandpa?" she asked.

"A girl that came here," answered the old man.

"May that girl always have long silky hair," the third lady said.

One by one the remaining ladies asked, and one by one they thanked the girl, granting her softness, grace, beautiful speech and that her mouth would exhale a wonderful aroma every time she smiled. The ladies who lived in the little blue house were fairies.

When they had finished thanking her, the girl ran back home. But when she arrived, her stepmother and stepsister were astonished to see her so beautiful, her forehead so luminous.

"Where have you been?" the stepmother yelled.

"Well, I was in a little house," she said, her voice faint with fear that they might beat her as they always did.

"Look here, I don't care where you were, but I do know that this very instant you are to take your sister back to that house. You will leave her there and come right back so you can wash the floor and cook the meal. Your story of the little chitlings means we have no dinner today. It is all your fault. Now go with your sister."

The girl took her sister and left her in front of the blue house where the little old man was sitting.

When the sister was about to go into the house, the little old man said, "Girl, bring me a glass of water."

"No, no," the sister answered. "I did not come here to give water to old men. That is not what I'm here for."

"I am very thirsty," the little old man said, but the sister didn't care. She heard the baby crying in the house, went in and smacked him on the bottom. She saw the dog moaning and kicked it. She heard the racket in the chicken coop and opened its doors. The chickens went into the kitchen and broke the glasses and the dishes. She kicked the cat and hit the parrot with the broom.

She was getting ready to leave, trampling on the flowers in the garden, when the seven ladies arrived. Frightened, the sister hid behind the gate.

But the parrot shrieked, "She's behind the gate! She's behind the gate!"

The fairies saw that the child was crying, that the dog was dead, the cat frightened, the flowers wilted and the chickens pecking and cackling in the kitchen. One by one, they each gave the sister something bad. One commanded that her feet grow so big that no shoe could fit her; another that her hair become straight and greasy. Another declared that she would have bad breath whenever she talked so no one would come near her, and another that she would grow a turkey's wattle on her forehead.

The sister ran back home. When her mother

saw her she was very scared. She took her to the doctor straight away so he could remove the turkey's wattle. But the doctor said that it was not possible, though he did suggest that she tie a bow on her forehead.

The mother tied the bow as she was told. But she also forced her stepdaughter to put a bandage on her forehead to conceal the star.

Around that time, the king announced that he would hold a party in the square so that the prince could choose his bride. He invited all the girls of the town to attend.

The stepmother and the sister went to the party, but they locked the girl in the house. The fairies also went. They took the parrot and left it on a bush close to the king and the prince.

When the king sat down, the parrot began to shriek, "Majesty! Majesty! Golden Star is in the house and Turkey Wattle is in the square!" The parrot repeated this again and again.

"I am tired of this," the king said finally. "What is it that this parrot wants to tell me?"

"Forgive us, your majesty," one of the fairies said. "It so happens that there is a very beautiful girl locked up in her house. Why don't you send for her?"

"Right away! Go and find her!"

One of the fairies took a carriage with four horses and went to the house. She touched the girl with a little wand and a beautiful dress appeared on her. She took the bandage off and rubbed her forehead until the star shone. Then they climbed into the carriage and returned to the square.

And no sooner did the prince see the girl than he fell in love with her and chose her for his bride.

WHITEFLOWER

RETOLD BY
MARGOT SILVA PÉREZ
ILLUSTRATED BY
IRENE SAVINO

Whiteflower was a very beautiful and magical girl. Though her father was a rich landowner, he had a very bad temper. He was so fierce that at times he resembled the devil himself. He loved Whiteflower so much that he did not let her go anywhere, nor did he want her ever to marry.

One day a young man arrived at the hacienda asking for work. When the old man saw him, young and good looking as he was, he immediately thought, "I don't want this one around here."

"There's no work here," he said.

At that moment, Whiteflower appeared and said in a voice as soft and gentle as a butterfly's, "Father, give him work, please."

The father was unable to deny Whiteflower anything because he adored her so.

"Come in," he said to the young man. "We will see what work we can find for you."

The young man came in, followed closely by the very beautiful Whiteflower.

"Whenever you wish to see me," she whispered to him, "rub this ring and I will appear immediately."

And she slipped the ring on his finger.

The old man meanwhile was speaking with the foreman of the hacienda.

"Foreman," he said. "Do me the favor of setting a trap for this man, so that he will leave as soon as tomorrow. I don't want him to stay."

"Don't worry," answered the foreman. "This one will not last here."

The foreman went to the young man straight away.

"You, what is your name?" he demanded.

"My name is Pedro, sir."

"All right, Pedro. You will clear this land, sow

the corn, harvest it, mill it and make me a loaf of bread the size of a cart wheel. By tomorrow." And he gave him a machete, a rake and a sickle, all made out of cardboard. Then he left him alone.

Seeing the immense land and meager tools, Pedro began to cry. "How am I to clear this much land with this stupid cardboard?" And he wiped the tears from his eyes with the ring.

In an instant Whiteflower appeared.

"What is the matter?"

"Well, almost everything," Pedro answered, drying his tears. And he told her what the foreman had told him to do.

"Hmmm. Don't worry, handsome Pedro. I will take care of this. Just put your head on my lap and sleep."

That is what Pedro did. In one second flat, Whiteflower had cleared the land, sowed the corn, harvested it, milled it and prepared a loaf of bread as large as a cart wheel.

"It's done, Pedro," she said. "Wake up."

Pedro woke up, got the bread and took it to the

foreman. The foreman took it to the owner. And the owner was furious.

"This is Whiteflower's doing," he said. "We will have to give him something truly difficult to do. Bring me two bags of corn seed, two bags of black beans and two sacks of rice."

The foreman brought the sacks and emptied them in a room. He mixed up all the seeds and then called Pedro and told him he had to separate them, seed by seed, and pile them neatly in corners of the room.

"Oh, my goodness!" Pedro said. "Now I'm in a real fix. How am I going to separate this mess seed by seed?"

He pressed one hand against the other in desperation, rubbing the ring, and immediately Whiteflower appeared.

"What now?" she asked.

And Pedro told her about the new job.

"Hmmm. Don't worry, handsome Pedro. I will take care of this, too. Put your head on my lap and sleep."

When Pedro was asleep, Whiteflower called out, "Little mice, little mice, come without delay. Come not tomorrow, but right away."

And thousands upon thousands of mice appeared.

"Put the beans over here, the corn over here and the rice over here, without mixing them up!" Whiteflower ordered, and the mice went to work separating the seeds and piling each kind in a corner.

In the morning, when the foreman came, the work was done.

"Boss, you will not believe it, but the work is done."

The father flew into a rage. He was furious.

"It cannot be. How could he have done it? Fine, but these are easy jobs. Now we will do something altogether different."

He then called over the other landowners and they all sat around a tree. They called Pedro and ordered him to climb the tree with a glass of water in his hand. If he spilled just one drop, they said, they would kill him.

Pedro was shaking with fear. He shook and he shook until, without thinking, he rubbed the ring against his shirt and immediately Whiteflower appeared and sat close to the tree.

As Pedro began to climb the tree with the glass of water, Whiteflower said in a whisper, "Freeze, freeze, freeze!"

The water froze in the glass and turned to ice, and Pedro spilled not a drop.

When Whiteflower's father and the landowners approached to see the glass of water, Whiteflower said in a whisper, "Melt, melt, melt!"

And the ice melted and turned to water again.

The father could not believe that Pedro had not spilled a single drop of water. He ordered him to climb the tree again and again. And one of those times a tiny drop of water spilled from the cup before turning to ice.

"There!" exclaimed the older man. "I saw a drop fall."

"No, Father, no. It was a tear," said Whiteflower. "Isn't that so, gentlemen?"

And she looked at all of them with her magic gaze.

"Yes, Miss Whiteflower," the landowners answered obediently. "It was a tear."

Whiteflower's father was so furious that he started to bite his nails. He knew that it was Whiteflower who was helping Pedro through his trials. So he decided that he would kill Pedro himself that night.

But Whiteflower overheard the old man and the foreman planning to kill Pedro while he was sleeping. She ran out to get two little gourds.

"Pedro," she told him, "take this little gourd and spit into it. I'll spit into this other one."

They spat and spat until the little gourds were full.

Whiteflower put small amounts of magic powder in them and left the gourds on their night tables.

"Let's go now, Pedro," she said. "My father wants to kill you. Go to the stable. There you will find two horses. One is fat and beautiful and its name is Wind. The other is thin and ugly and its name is Thought. Bring back only Thought."

But Pedro decided that he liked the fat and beautiful horse better, so he mounted it and took the thin and ugly one to Whiteflower.

"Oh, Pedro!" said Whiteflower, and she mounted her horse. They ran away at a full gallop, but of course Pedro lagged behind because thought runs faster than the wind.

Meanwhile the old man and the foreman knocked on the door of Pedro's room to see whether he was still asleep.

"Pedro!" said the foreman.

The saliva in the gourd answered, "Yes, sir?"

"He's not asleep yet," said the old man. "Let's wait a minute. I will go and see if Whiteflower is sleeping."

He went and knocked on Whiteflower's door.

"Whiteflower!"

The saliva in the other gourd answered, "Yes, Father?"

And they went on like this for a while.

"Pedro!"

"Yes, sir?"

"Whiteflower!"

"Yes, Father?"

Until the saliva began to dry in the little gourds and the voices became fainter.

Then the foreman went into Pedro's room to kill him and realized that there was no one in the room.

"They have escaped, sir!" the foreman cried out, and both went to the stable to find horses, but Wind and Thought were missing. So they mounted the two other horses, Typhoon and Hurricane, and set out at a full gallop.

Pedro and Whiteflower were already far away, but Pedro's horse was slower and Whiteflower had to wait for him. At one point Whiteflower looked back and saw her father and the foreman almost upon them.

"Oh, Whiteflower! Your father is going to kill me!" cried Pedro in fear.

"Don't worry, Pedro. I will take care of it."

Whiteflower took a pin she had stuck in her clothes and threw it behind her.

Immediately a thicket of thorns grew up on the road. The enormous thorns got into the horses' hooves, making it difficult for them to continue. But the foreman and the father dug their spurs into their horses and with bleeding legs they managed to get through. Soon they had almost caught up once again.

"Whiteflower! Do something!" Pedro cried out.

Whiteflower took a little piece of soap she had in her pocket and threw it behind her. The road immediately turned into a huge mud puddle. The horses slipped and fell and it was impossible to mount them again.

Whiteflower and Pedro kept at a full gallop until they came to a small chapel.

"They'll be here any minute," said Whiteflower. "We'll have to disguise ourselves. I will be the virgin and you will be the hermit of the chapel. Whatever they ask you, you must only answer, 'Ding, dong, oh, to mass they go!' You must do exactly as I say."

And so it was. The mud dried up and the foreman and the father once again mounted Typhoon and Hurricane and in a second they had arrived at the chapel.

"Dear hermit, have you seen a young woman and a young man coming this way?"

"Ding, dong, oh, to mass they go!" answered Pedro, truly frightened.

"No, I don't want to go to mass," said the father. "I'm asking whether you have seen a young man and a very beautiful girl called Whiteflower come by."

"Ding, dong, oh, to mass they go!"

"I told you already. I don't want to go to mass. I'm looking for Whiteflower, my daughter."

"Ding, dong, ding, dong, to mass they go!"

"I don't want to hear any more ding, dong. Tell me whether you have seen my daughter Whiteflower or not!"

There was nothing the father could do. Pedro kept on with his ding, dong until the old man gave up and left.

"What will we do when they come back?" Pedro asked Whiteflower.

"You'll be a farmer and I'll be the farmer's wife. We'll sell tomatoes there by the bend on the road."

When the father came back he asked them, "Good morning, dear farmers. Did a young man and a young woman come through here?"

"Tomatoes. Do you want to buy tomatoes?"

"Tomatoes. Red, beautiful, cheap tomatoes."

"No, I don't want tomatoes," the father answered angrily. "I want to know whether you have seen a young man and a young woman."

But there was nothing he could do. Tomatoes and more tomatoes was all the talk the old man heard, until he got fed up and left, furious.

"What will we do, Whiteflower, when your father and the foreman come again?" Pedro asked. "We have already tried everything."

"Don't worry," said Whiteflower. "You will be a little bird and I will be a little bird and we'll go to that tree and start singing."

And when the father and the foreman came by, the two birds began their song in the tree.

The old man sat under the tree and told the foreman, "Foreman, we have been fooled. That man took my daughter with him. Let's go home and let her live her own life."

And so it was. The old man and the foreman went back to the hacienda and Whiteflower and Pedro went far away, and they were very happy.

And ding, dong clover, this story is over.

CROOKED FOOT
THE DWARF

RETOLD BY
RAFAEL RIVERO ORAMAS
ILLUSTRATED BY
HEINZ ROSE

I n a clearing in a forest surrounded by high
mountains lived dwarves who spent their lives
happily working in the mines and the fields.

No one ever bothered them because the high
mountains shielded them from the rest of the
world. Nobody knew of the existence of their little
town.

One day a giant appeared. Because he was so
tall, he could see over the mountains.

The dwarves fled in terror and took refuge in
the thickest part of the forest. The giant tore down
their houses, trampled their fields and ate all the
food they had in storage.

"Yum," he said, looking at the small fields that
remained. "All this is really well kept. There is

enough food to last me a long time. I think I'll stay here."

And he went to the forest, tore out some trees, roots and all, and built himself a house as big as the dwarves' whole town had once been.

The giant lived there happily for a long time, while the dwarves hid in the forest and went hungry.

One day, the most daring of the dwarves decided to go and see if they could force the giant to abandon the place.

But the giant stood on his toes and shouted, his voice like thunder, "*Ahhrgh*! Stupid dwarves, get out of here!"

He swung his arms around as though he was shooing away flies, and the dwarves had to run back to the forest again.

The dwarves were sad, but they got used to living under the trees. Then one day a little foreign dwarf arrived and wondered why they were living that way, so frightened, so far away from home.

The foreigner was called Crooked Foot.

When they told him the story of the giant, he laughed long and hard.

"How can so many dwarves be afraid of a single giant?" he asked.

"Well, you don't know him," said one. "He's terrible. He's taller than the tallest mountain."

Crooked Foot laughed again.

"Don't be fools! I'll bet I can bring him down all by myself, no matter how big or how horrid he might be."

The dwarves looked at one another and thought to themselves, "Is Crooked Foot an idiot, or what? Is he half crazy?"

And they began to watch him.

Crooked Foot did not look like someone capable of defeating a giant. He was small like the rest of them. He was neither fat nor thin and he did not look particularly wise, either. He did, however, keep laughing and making fun of the dwarves, insisting that he could defeat the giant.

Finally the dwarves could not stand it anymore.

"If you are so brave, why don't you do as you say?"

"Hah! So you don't think I can? Just watch me tomorrow."

Very early the next day, Crooked Foot went to the giant's house. The giant was sleeping. Crooked Foot began to pound at the door and made a lot of noise. The giant got up, startled, and went to see what was going on.

When he found the little dwarf at his door, he howled and waved his arms around to frighten him off, just as he had done with the others.

But Crooked Foot did not move.

The giant went into his house in a huff and came out with a large white quartz stone. "Look carefully," he told Crooked Foot, and he threw the stone against the ground. The stone turned into dust.

"This is what I could do to you," said the giant. "So go away and don't bother me."

Crooked Foot guffawed.

The giant looked at him and frowned. Then he took a black stone from the ground and pressed it between his large hands until three drops fell from the stone.

"That's stone juice," the giant roared. "Get out of here if you don't want your juices squeezed."

"Hah, hah! Don't be such a fool, big giant," Crooked Foot laughed. "I can do that, too. Just wait and you will see."

And, turning his back on the giant, he started for the forest, where the surprised dwarves were watching him.

"Get me a little yucca starch and a pile of tarred straw," he said.

The dwarves, having seen Crooked Foot's courage in front of the giant, ran to get what he asked for.

Crooked Foot put the yucca starch in his pocket and went to the stream where he moistened the pile of tarred straw and put that in his pocket, too.

Then he took a white quartz stone and a black stone and went back to the giant.

"Look closely," he told the giant. "This is the same kind of stone you made into dust."

Faster than a mosquito can blink, he exchanged the white quartz stone for the starch. He swung his arm and threw it against the ground. All that was left on the ground was a stain of white dust.

The giant opened his eyes wide, surprised to see someone so small with enough strength to turn a white quartz stone into dust.

"Now you will see the next one," Crooked Foot said.

He took the black stone and, faster than a fly can blink, he exchanged it for a piece of tarred straw. Then he began to squeeze it between his fists, feigning tremendous effort, until a few drops fell out.

"That's stone juice," he said.

The giant was flabbergasted.

"I want to be your friend," he said, shaking hands with Crooked Foot. "I like strong men and I want to invite you to have breakfast with me."

Crooked Foot accepted the invitation and they went into the house, laughing and chatting.

"Well," the giant said. "I don't have servants,

but because we are buddies you will help me set the table."

"My pleasure," said Crooked Foot.

"Well, then, while I go to look for the barrel of milk that I have below, you go to the kitchen and bring the cornmeal rolls that are cooking on the stove."

And each of them went in his own direction.

In the kitchen Crooked Foot found himself in a predicament. The stove was terribly high and only after fetching a ladder did he manage to reach the cornmeal rolls. They were enormous.

With a huge effort he took one down and, rolling it like a cart wheel, he took it to the table. He puffed and wiped the sweat from his forehead. Then he went back to the kitchen and, with the same effort, took another cornmeal roll.

He was quite proud of himself, spinning the second cornmeal roll along, when he suddenly bumped against the dining-room door. He fell, and the enormous cornmeal roll fell right on top of him.

And there he stayed, crushed like a cockroach.

Crooked Foot tried to free himself, but to no avail. The weight of the roll was crushing him and the heat was burning him, but he did not dare cry for help.

He was struggling to get out when the giant came in with the large barrel of milk on his shoulder.

"What's this, Crooked Foot? What happened to you?" he asked, surprised.

"Ah, my friend! I suffer from rheumatism and, as they say, hot cornmeal rolls are good medicine."

"But it's not right," said the giant, annoyed, "to use the cornmeal we are going to eat this way."

And while he was talking, he lifted the cornmeal roll that was crushing the dwarf and put it on the table.

"Well, then, let's eat," said Crooked Foot, standing up and walking to the table as if nothing had happened.

They had almost finished eating when the

giant's nose began to tickle and his eyes began to water. Before he could stop himself, he sneezed.

It was like a cyclone. The house shook, the chairs and everything on the table flew around. Crooked Foot flew, too.

When things had calmed down, the dwarf was hanging from the ceiling with one hand on a beam. The giant was looking at him.

"What are you doing up there, Crooked Foot?"

"You have no manners, big giant," the dwarf answered, irritated. "How dare you sneeze at the table? I am going to tear this beam out and break it over your head."

The giant was scared and ran to help Crooked Foot down from the ceiling.

"No, don't do that! I'm your friend."

"Friend? I can't be friends with such an ill-behaved giant."

"Wow!" thought the giant. "This darned dwarf could kill me any minute."

So, when Crooked Foot wasn't watching, the giant escaped. And he never came back.

The dwarves returned from the forest, rebuilt their town and lived happily ever after.

As for Crooked Foot? He went out and got himself a boot.

THE BASIL POT

RETOLD BY
PASCUALA CORONA
ILLUSTRATED BY
MARÍA FERNANDA OLIVER

There once was a very poor shoemaker who lived in front of the palace. He had three daughters.

The girls had a potted basil plant in the window of their house and each one of them watered it on alternate days. All three were very beautiful and one day when the king went out on the balcony of his palace, he saw the eldest of the sisters watering the plant and said, "Young girl, young girl who waters the pot. Can you count the number of leaves or not?"

The girl, distressed at being addressed by the king and not knowing what to say, closed the window.

The next day it was the second sister's turn to water the plant. The king went out to the balcony and, as he'd done the previous day, said, "Young girl, young girl who waters the pot. Can you count the number of leaves or not?"

The girl, embarrassed at being talked to by the king, pretended she was deaf and went back inside.

On the third day the youngest sister went to water the plant. The king, who was already on the balcony, said, "Young girl, young girl who waters the pot. Can you count the number of leaves or not?"

And the girl, who was very bright, answered, "Does your majesty, my king and lord, know how many rays shine from the sun?"

The king was taken by surprise by the girl and, embarrassed because he couldn't answer, he ran back into his room. After much thinking, it occurred to him that because the girl was so poor he should send a servant to walk down the street shouting that he would exchange grapes for kisses.

The girl couldn't imagine what this was about, but she went down and gave the servant the kiss he asked for in exchange for the grapes.

The next morning when she went to the window to water the plant, the king was already on his balcony. Upon seeing her he said, "Young girl, you who water the pot, you who have kissed my servant, can you count the number of leaves or not?"

The girl became so angry that she slammed the window and went back inside, determined never to water the plant again.

The king fell sick with love. His doctor, seeing that he was unable to cure him, sent for all the doctors in the kingdom to see which of them could relieve the king of his illness.

The girl, who was waiting for a chance to get even, dressed up as a doctor and went to the palace pulling a donkey by its halter.

When she was in the presence of the king she said, "Your majesty, if you wish to recover from your illness, you must kiss the tail of my donkey and tomorrow morning you must go out on your balcony and feel the first rays of the sun."

The king, anxious to find a cure, did what the doctor said, and after kissing the tail of the donkey, he went to bed and fell asleep.

Very early the next morning he stepped out on his balcony. The girl was waiting for him and while she watered her plant, she said, "Does your majesty, my king and lord, having kissed the tail of my donkey, know how many rays shine from the sun?"

The king, realizing how thoroughly the girl had fooled him, was very angry and sent for the shoemaker.

As soon as the good man arrived the king said, "Neighbor shoemaker, on the third hour of the third day you will bring me your three daughters. I command that the youngest one come to me bathed and not bathed, her hair at once combed and not combed, on horseback and not on horseback. I warn you, if you don't comply, you'll be risking your life."

The poor shoemaker went home very sad and told his daughters what the king had commanded. The two elder ones did nothing but cry, but the youngest said, "Don't worry, Daddy. You'll see how I fix everything."

And so it was. At three o'clock on the third day the shoemaker came to the palace with his three daughters. The two older ones went first, and a little behind followed the youngest one mounted on a donkey, with one foot in the air and the other touching the floor. She was dirty on one side and on the other spanking clean, half her hair was in a tangle and the other combed into a perfect braid.

The king saw that they had fulfilled his command, gave up and said to the girl, "As a reward for your shrewdness you may take from the palace whatever you wish." Then he went to take his afternoon nap.

This was just what the girl was waiting for.

She summoned four page boys and had them carefully take the king to her house.

You can imagine the king's surprise when he woke up in a poor and unfamiliar house!

The first thing he did was to call his lackeys, his pages and his guards. Instead, however, it was the girl who came and said, "Your royal highness, my king and my lord, you were what I liked most from your palace and thus I have brought you to my home."

And the king, seeing that with this girl he would always end up losing, married her.

María Tolete

RETOLD BY
RAFAEL OLIVARES FIGUEROA
ILLUSTRATED BY
IRENE SAVINO

A ragged, hungry young girl showed up one day at the gates of the main building of an hacienda. The people who lived there gave her something to eat and to drink. But she came back the next day, and the next, and the one after that. Without anyone noticing, the young girl stayed around, always quiet, moving from one corner to another.

One afternoon the boys of the hacienda asked her what her name was and she answered in a tiny voice, "María."

And the boys laughed and danced around her, making fun of her.

"María, María Tolete! María, María Tolete!"

One night, under the full moon, the son of the lady who owned the hacienda was getting ready to go to a dance when María Tolete appeared to him in his room.

"Take me with you," she said.

The young man stiffened in surprise.

"What's this? Do you think you can go to the dance with me?" he shouted. "Go back to your corner. Watch out or I'll hit you with this vest!"

When the young man had left for the dance, María Tolete went to the well in the forest, bathed in its waters and perfumed herself with the herbs that grew there. She went back to the house, put on a beautiful dress – one that belonged to the owner's daughter – and put her hair up in a bun.

At the dance all were amazed at the beauty of this young woman no one knew. Men fought with each other over the right to dance with her, and the son from the hacienda couldn't take his eyes off her.

"Where do you come from?" he finally asked her.

"Oh, I come from very far away," María Tolete answered. "I come from the city of Vest-hit."

The young man was so spellbound by her beauty that he didn't notice anything else.

When the young man returned to his home he couldn't stop talking about the unknown young woman he had seen at the dance. In the days that followed, he looked for her all over the hacienda and in the surrounding towns but was unable to find her. He became very sad.

On a moonless night a fortnight later, the young man was invited to another dance. As on the first occasion, María Tolete appeared in his room and said in her faint voice, "Take me with you."

The young man again yelled at her. "How can you think about going to a dance with me? Go to your corner, or I'll give you a slash with the blade of my knife!"

When the young man had left, María Tolete ran to the well, took a bath, perfumed herself, put on another one of the dresses belonging to the owner's daughter, and put her hair up in a bun.

All at the dance were once more dazzled by the beauty of this unknown young woman. The owner's son approached her and sighed. "Tell me, where do you come from?"

"Oh, I come from a place far away. I come from the town of Knifeblade-slash," answered María Tolete, but the young man failed to notice anything, because he had fallen in love.

When he arrived home he could not tire from praising the unknown young woman at the dance. In the days that followed, he searched all over the hacienda and the surrounding towns for her, but to no avail. And he became even sadder.

Fifteen days later, on a night when the moon was full, the young man was invited to another dance. For the third time María Tolete appeared in his room and asked in her faint voice, "Take me with you."

And he yelled at her for the third time. "What's this? How can you even think of going to the ball with me? Go to your corner. If you don't, I'll give you a smack with my shoe!"

After the young man had left again, María Tolete dressed marvelously and went off to the dance. All were dazzled by her beauty. The young man danced with her, whispered loving words in her ear and gave her a ring.

And for the third time he asked her, "Tell me, where are you from?"

"Oh, I come from a distant place, very distant," answered María Tolete. "I come from the town of Shoe-smack."

But because the young man had almost lost his mind out of his love for her, he paid no attention to the meaning of her words.

When he went back home, the young man woke up everybody to tell them about the beauty of the unknown young woman. The next day he looked for her all over the hacienda and the surrounding towns but was unable to find her. He was so sad that he became ill. There was no medicine to heal him, nor could prayers help him recover his strength.

Then María Tolete asked the lady of the hacienda to allow her to make a hot maize drink for the sick man. The lady became furious. "How can you think that my son will want the maize drink that you make, girl! He likes the drinks his mother makes him."

But María Tolete insisted until the lady, annoyed, finally gave her permission. María Tolete prepared the thick hot maize drink and, without anyone noticing, placed the ring inside it.

While he was drinking, the young man sighed, "What a tasty hot maize drink, Mother." Upon finding the ring he asked, "Who prepared this drink?"

"María Tolete made it," the lady of the hacienda answered. "Why do you ask?" But before the young man could answer, María Tolete appeared wearing a beautiful dress, clean, perfumed and with her hair up in a bun.

In an instant the young man was cured. And he married her.

They lived happily ever after, joined in laughter, drinking maize the rest of their days.

THE GRIFFIN

RETOLD BY
CARMEN HENY
ILLUSTRATED BY
HEINZ ROSE

Once there was a king who had an only daughter whom he loved very much. But the king was sad because his daughter was always ill. He had consulted with all the sages and medicine people of the kingdom, but no one could find out what was wrong with her.

One day an old woman dressed in rags came to the palace. The king thought that she had come to beg, but such was not the case.

"If your daughter eats the apples from the farthest orchard, she'll get well," the little old woman said, and then she disappeared.

So the king let all in his kingdom know that the one who brought apples from the most distant orchard would be the one to marry his daughter.

The owner of the farthest orchard was an old

farm hand who had three sons: Teodomiro, the oldest; Nicanor, the middle son; and Juan, the youngest.

The old man told Teodomiro, "Go tomorrow. Pick the most beautiful apples from the orchard and take them to the palace. If the king's daughter gets well, you will also be king."

Early the next morning Teodomiro filled a basket with the best apples and began his journey to the palace. He had walked many miles when he met a little old lady by the bend of the road.

"What do you have in that basket, young man?" she asked.

Teodomiro, who was pretentious and foolish, answered, "Frogs' legs."

"So be it and so they may remain," the little old lady told him kindly.

Teodomiro finally arrived at the palace and announced to the guards that he had the apples for the king's daughter. They told him to come right in and the king himself led him to the princess's room.

Can you imagine their surprise when his basket

was uncovered and it revealed only frogs' legs? Furious, the king kicked Teodomiro out of the palace.

When he got back home he told his father all that had happened and the old farm hand called Nicanor, who was brighter, and told him, "Go early and take the apples to the king's daughter. If she becomes healthy, you will also be king."

Nicanor did so.

At a bend in the road he ran into the same little old woman.

"What have you in your basket?" she inquired.

And Nicanor, who was full of himself as well as a joker, answered, "Little pigs' feet."

"So be it, and so they may remain," said the little old woman, smiling.

Nicanor arrived at the palace feeling like he had already been crowned king and announced that he was bringing apples for the princess. By now the guards were not so confident and didn't let him in. After much pleading they opened the door with caution and took him to the room of the princess.

But when he uncovered the basket, all they found were pigs' feet!

The king was furious and had him kicked out of the palace.

When he got home Nicanor told his father what had happened. Then Juan, the youngest, asked his father for permission to take the apples to the princess.

"No way," said the old farm hand. "If your two brothers failed, what will you achieve, being the fool that you are?"

But Juan insisted and pleaded for so long that his father tired of it and let him go.

Juan got up at dawn, took the most beautiful apples from the orchard and started walking. Just like his brothers, he found the little old woman by the bend in the road and sat down with her to rest.

"What do you have in the basket?" asked the little old woman.

"Apples to cure the king's daughter," answered Juan.

"So be it, and so they may remain," said the little old lady, and she disappeared.

Juan kept going, happy and confident. He arrived at the gates of the palace, but this time there was no way they would let him in. Finally, after much pleading, they opened the gates.

"What are you bringing?" said the king.

"Apples from the farthest orchard to cure the princess," Juan replied.

"If you fool me," warned the king, "you will not leave this place alive."

Juan asked to be taken to the princess's room and in front of the king uncovered his basket. In it were the juiciest and most beautiful apples. As soon as the princess ate one she jumped out of bed and embraced her father.

The king was happy. He soon remembered that he had to give the princess away in marriage to Juan, who seemed like a fool to him, and he began to come up with excuses.

"Before you can marry my daughter," he told Juan, "you must bring me a feather from the tail of the Griffin."

The next day, Juan went on his way. At nightfall

he found himself close to a large house. Because it was so dark and he was so tired, he knocked on the door. The owner asked him where he was going and Juan told him that he was going to take a feather from the tail of the Griffin so he could marry the king's daughter.

"Well, then, come in and sleep here," the owner answered. "I would like to ask a favor of you. People say that the Griffin is all-knowing. I have lost the key to the trunk where I keep the things I treasure. Could you ask him where it is?"

"I will do that," said Juan, and he went to bed.

He got up early and went on his way again. The following night he arrived at a large estate and knocked on the door. The owner asked him where he was going and Juan told him the story of the Griffin.

"Come in and sleep here," answered the owner. "Could you do me a favor and ask the Griffin for medicine to cure my daughter who is getting sicker and sicker by the day? Nothing is helping to make her better."

"I will do so," said Juan.

The next morning he continued on his way and at noon he came to a great lake he would have to cross. There was no boat, however – only a very large man who carried people from one shore to the other. The man asked him where he was going.

"I'm going to see the Griffin," said Juan.

"Oh!" sighed the man. "When you find him, can you ask him what I can do so I don't have to remain here for the rest of my life, endlessly carrying people from one shore to the other?"

"I will do so," said Juan.

When he finally came to the Griffin's cave, he found, to his great surprise, the same little old woman from the road standing by the door.

"What are you doing here, boy? Don't you know that the Griffin eats people? He swallows each and every soul who comes here in one gulp."

"I've come to take a feather from his tail so I can marry the king's daughter," said Juan. "And also to ask him three things. Where is the key to the trunk in the big house where I spent my first night? What medicine will cure the daughter of the owner of the estate where I spent the second night? And what does the big man of the lake have to do to stop carrying people from one shore to the other?"

"Young man, don't think about asking him anything. Don't dare breathe when he is here. I will ask him all those things for you. Pay attention to his answers. Don't get mixed up," answered the little old woman. "Now, curl up under his bed. He will be here any minute. Don't be afraid of the noises he makes, as if the whole mountain is shaking. When you hear that he is fast asleep, after he has answered all my questions, go out very quietly, and with a single good pull rip out a feather. Now you know."

It wasn't long before a racket was heard. It was the huge bird returning to his nest, famished as always.

As soon as he opened the door he yelled, "I SMELL HUMAN FLESH! Old woman, where is the Christian soul I will have for dinner today?"

"You said Christian soul? What Christian soul?" answered the little old woman. "No one has been here today, though I did prepare you a tasty meal."

The bird gorged himself on everything the little old woman put before him, without realizing that she had put little herbs in his food that made him terribly tired. He went to bed and fell asleep.

The little nap didn't last long, however, because the bird was very canny and soon woke and cried, "Old woman, I SMELL HUMAN FLESH!"

"Simmer down, my bird," the little old woman said, stroking his head. "Yes, it is true. A few days ago a Christian came by asking where the key to the trunk in the big house could be found."

"Ah, what a dodo. Doesn't he realize that the key is under that big piece of lumber where the firewood is kept?"

"The man also asked what medicine was needed to cure the daughter of the owner of the big estate, as she is so sick and no one can make her feel better."

"Ah, what a dummy. Doesn't he know that under the mamón bush there is a stone and under the stone there is a toad that has three of his daughter's hairs caught in one of its legs? If she picks them off, she will get well."

"Lastly, he asked what the big man at the lake can do so he doesn't have to carry people from one shore to the other anymore," said the little old woman.

"What a fool! All he has to do is to drop the person he is carrying in the middle of the lake and he will be free."

Finally, the Griffin, tired from so much talking, fell asleep and began to snore. In one leap, Juan pulled the feather out of the Griffin's tail and ran out of the cave. Outside he bade the little old woman goodbye and started walking as fast as he could, just in case the bird should wake up.

When he arrived at the lake the big man asked him, "What news do you have for me?"

"I will tell you when we get to the other shore," answered Juan. When he had crossed to the other shore, he said, "You should let go of your next passenger in the middle of the lake, and that will mark the end of your travails."

When Juan arrived at the estate, the owner asked him, "What news do you have?"

"Take me to your daughter's room and you will see."

The owner of the estate did as he was told. Juan carried the girl to the mamón bush and raised the stone. The toad was there with the girl's three hairs. She took the hairs and raced in to embrace her father, cured as she was for life.

"What can I pay you for this?" asked the overjoyed estate owner.

"Nothing," said Juan. But the estate owner gave him goats, sheep and much money, and with all that wealth Juan was on his way.

At the door of the big house the owner asked him, "What news have you got?"

Juan went straight to the firewood shed and lifted the big piece of lumber. Together they opened the trunk. Juan had never seen so much gold and so many jewels. The thankful owner gave him a load of gold, but for Juan the greatest treasure was the Griffin's feather.

Finally he was back at the palace once again. Nobody could believe that this was the same Juan as before. When the king saw everything – the sheep, the goats, the money and the gold, he asked Juan where he had got it all. And Juan answered that the Griffin had given him everything he had asked for.

It occurred to the king that he should also visit the Griffin, and he immediately set off on his journey. When he came to the lake, it turned out that he was the first person to appear since Juan had passed through. The big man took him and let him fall right in the middle of the lake, and there he stayed.

And Juan married the princess and they lived happily ever after.

This is where the tale ends. If you wish to hear another, just go and ask Mother or Father.

OCELOT, JAGUAR AND LION

RETOLD BY
RAFAEL RIVERO ORAMAS
ILLUSTRATED BY
MARÍA FERNANDA OLIVER

There once was a widower who had two children, Pedro and Elena. All three lived in a little house close to the mountain. Not far from there lived a young woman who gave honey wafers to the children each time they passed by her house.

"Do marry that young woman," Pedro and Elena told their father. "She's very good and gives us honey wafers."

And the father always answered, "My little ones, first the honey, then the vinegar." But the children insisted so much that they convinced him, and he finally married the young woman.

For a while they were happy, but then the woman began to complain about the children. One night she told her husband that she wanted him to abandon them someplace far away. The man refused. The woman repeated the same thing every day, until in the end the man said yes, he would take them to the mountain and he would leave them there.

But Pedro was a bright boy, and he had noticed the change in the woman's behavior toward them. He overheard the conversation that evening and in the morning, when his father asked them to go to the mountain with him in search of firewood, he took along a can full of ashes.

As they were making their way to the mountain, Pedro spread ashes on the trail. While the children were busy gathering firewood, the father stealthily walked away and abandoned them. When Pedro and Elena realized that they were alone, they followed the trail of ashes and arrived home without any trouble at all.

The father was very happy to see them, but the woman was extremely cross and ordered her husband to take them much farther away.

The next day at dawn, the father woke the chil-

dren to take them on a hunting trip. This time the children filled the can with corn. And on the way they let the corn fall on the trail. When they were halfway up the mountain, the father told them to stay there while he went hunting for capybaras. And he did not come back for them.

As night began to fall, Pedro and Elena decided to take the trail back home, following the grains of corn. But the corn had disappeared. They realized then that the birds had eaten it. They were lost on that dark mountain.

Pedro climbed the tallest tree and from there he could see a light. They walked toward it until they came to a little house. They crept up very carefully and noticed that there was an old woman inside frying slices of meat. Making no noise, Pedro went in and snuck close to the old woman, who was blind in one eye. He began to steal the meat.

The old woman thought the cat was stealing the food and said, "Little cat keen. You eat the fat and leave me the lean."

Pedro filled his hat with food and took it to his

sister who was waiting for him close to the little house.

Pedro explained to Elena how he had taken the food. She wanted to go back for more herself. Pedro didn't want her to, because she always got the giggles, but in the end he agreed.

Elena did as her brother had done. She began to steal slices of meat, and the old woman, thinking that it was the cat, said, "Little cat keen. You eat the fat and leave me the lean."

Elena couldn't help it, and she giggled out loud. Then the old woman said, "Oh, you beautiful children, come here!"

She took them into a dark room and fed them every day to make them fat. And every day she would ask them to push their little fingers through a little hole in the door, so she could feel how much they had fattened.

Pedro found a little mouse and took off its tail. Each day, when the old woman asked them to show her their little fingers, they would push the tail of the mouse through the hole.

When the old woman felt the tail she always said, "Oh, my little children, you are so skinny."

Once, while Pedro and Elena were playing, they lost the mouse tail, and when the old woman came they had to put their fingers through.

"Oh, my little children," she said, surprised, "from one day to the next you have become fat!"

She took them out of the dark room immediately and lit the oven.

"My beautiful little children, go now and fetch me some firewood," she told them.

Out went Pedro and Elena, and in the forest they found a little old woman who asked them what they were doing. The children explained that the old woman in the little house had sent them to look for firewood.

"Oh, that woman is a very bad witch who eats children," said the little old woman.

"A witch!" said Pedro and Elena, frightened. But the little old woman put them at ease.

"When you go back with the firewood she will ask you to dance in front of the oven. Don't do it.

Tell her that you don't know how to dance and that she should show you first. When the witch is dancing, push her into the oven. Once she has turned into ashes, make three piles and call out, "Ocelot, jaguar and lion! Three dogs will appear and they will be your friends and guardians. Whenever you are in trouble, just call them and they will appear."

The children thanked the little old woman and returned to the witch's house. Everything happened exactly as the little old woman had told them. The old woman told them to dance and they said, "No, old mother. Why don't you dance first so we can learn? We do not know how to dance."

The old woman began to dance in front of them and they pushed her into the oven.

They formed three piles of her ashes and called out, "Ocelot, jaguar and lion!"

Three dogs appeared, and they all went on their way.

They walked and walked until they arrived in a deserted town. In the doorway of a house they found yet another woman.

"What are you doing here all by yourself?" asked the children.

And she explained that all the townsfolk had left, fleeing from a great seven-headed serpent. This serpent would come out of the river every day and take a young woman and eat her. On this very day it was to be the king's daughter's turn, as she was the only young woman left in the town.

In his despair the king had placed an advertisement in the papers stating that whoever could save his daughter would be the one to marry her.

Upon hearing this, Pedro took to the river. He saw the princess sitting on a rock waiting for the serpent. At that very instant a fearsome seven-headed serpent emerged from the river and Pedro called out, "Ocelot, jaguar and lion!"

Instantly three dogs appeared. They helped Pedro fight the serpent and kill it.

The king's daughter thanked him and ran to her father to tell him what had happened. Meanwhile, Pedro cut the seven tongues off the seven heads of the serpent and walked to the town.

Soon a man came by the shore of the river and saw the dead serpent. He cut off the seven heads and went to the king's house.

"It is I who killed the serpent and here in this bag is my proof," he said. He opened his bag and seven heads came rolling out. "I have come to marry the princess."

But the princess insisted that this man wasn't the one that had killed the serpent and that she would not marry him.

"You have to marry him because I've given my word," the king said. "I promised that whoever saved you would marry you."

The wedding was prepared, with a big party. On the day of the wedding Pedro went to the king.

"How can this man prove that he killed the serpent?" he asked.

The stranger took out the seven heads and made them roll on the floor once again.

"Open the mouths of the seven heads," Pedro said.

When the man opened them, people could see there were no tongues.

"Where are the seven tongues?" Pedro asked.

"The ants ate them," the imposter said.

Then Pedro took the seven tongues out of his pocket and showed them to the king.

The king threw the man in jail, and the princess and Pedro were married and were happy.

And I went home to tell the story.

The Talking Bird, the Singing Tree and the Fountain of Gold

RETOLD BY
CARMEN HENY
ILLUSTRATED BY
IRENE SAVINO

There once was a king who had never married. He lived in a very luxurious palace, yet his favorite pastime was to go hunting in the forest. He went to hunt one day and as he passed a village, he heard voices coming from a humble little house that belonged to a widow and her three daughters.

"If you could marry anyone you wanted, who would it be?" one of the girls asked her sisters.

"I would marry the king's baker, because that way I would always have bread," said the eldest.

"I would marry his cook," said the middle sister. "That way I would never be hungry."

But the youngest one, who was the brightest, said, "Well, I would marry the king himself."

The king was very curious about what he had

heard and went into the house to meet the sisters. He thought the youngest was the most beautiful being he had ever laid eyes on and so he said, "Your wishes will come true."

Immediately he sent for the royal baker and the royal cook, and he married them to the two older sisters while he married the youngest one.

A few months later the king's first child was born – a boy. The sisters were very jealous.

"Why do we have to live with the baker and the cook while she lives in the palace and has it all?" they would say.

Even though the king constantly showered the older sisters with beautiful gifts, their jealousy grew.

The oldest decided to steal the baby boy. She placed him in a basket and put the basket in the river so it would carry him far away. However, the basket just floated to a bend in the river where it got stuck.

An elderly couple of farmers who had no children of their own lived in a house nearby and were in the habit of going to the river in the evenings.

The farmer found the basket and showed it to his wife. Both were very happy when they discovered the baby, and so they raised the boy.

Soon another boy was born in the palace. The king, who was greatly worried about the disappearance of his firstborn, put guards everywhere. But it never occurred to him that he should watch his wife's sisters. The second sister, who was growing more and more envious, decided to do exactly as her older sister had done. She took the baby, placed him in a basket and launched him down river. The two farmers, who kept coming to the river in the evenings, again found the basket.

Now they had two sons.

The king was so distressed that he became sad and thin.

Soon a girl was born and the king had security tightened, without ever thinking that his own sisters-in-law were the ones stealing his children. A few days after her birth, the little girl disappeared. The same thing happened to her that had happened to her brothers.

Desperate, the king offered a reward to anyone who could give him information about his children.

The oldest sister approached him.

"Majesty, we have never wanted to tell you for fear you wouldn't believe us, but our sister is an ogre. She has always eaten baby meat."

The king could not believe it. He was horrified and ordered his sister-in-law not to speak. But little by little, when the children didn't appear, he began to think that it was true – that he had married an ogre. And so he commanded that his wife be put in a cage.

Years went by. The three children grew up among the trees and the flowers on the small farm. Over time, the old couple died and the three were left alone.

One day they heard about a magic mountain where there was a talking bird, a singing tree and a fountain of gold.

"If we had these wonderful things we wouldn't feel so lonely," said the oldest boy. "I am going to look for them."

"Don't go," the girl said. "They say that whoever goes up that mountain is turned into stone and never returns."

But her brother insisted. "Don't worry about me," he answered. "I'm not going to turn into stone."

He gave her a knife with a shiny blade.

"Look at this knife every night. The day the blade becomes cloudy, it will be a sign that something has happened to me."

Then he saddled his horse and left.

At the foot of the mountain he found a little old man.

"Don't go up that wretched mountain," the little old man said. "Many have tried and, I tell you, no one has ever come back."

But the young man insisted.

Then the old man said, "I am going to throw this marble. Wherever it lands, climb off your horse and start walking. Be careful never to look back no matter what you may hear, because if you do, you will turn into stone and you will never again leave the place."

They said goodbye and the little old man wished him luck.

Meanwhile, on the farm, the girl looked at the knife every night and every night she went to bed peacefully because the blade was still shining.

But one night when she took it out, she saw that the blade was cloudy.

"You see why I didn't want him to leave?" she cried to her other brother. "Now he must be dead. Or maybe he has turned to stone."

"I will go to look for him," the other brother said. "Nothing will happen to me."

The girl wept and tried to discourage him. But he mounted his horse and gave her a rosary.

"Pray for me every night. If at any time the beads stick together, it will mean that something has happened to me."

Feeling sad, she prayed the rosary every evening, until one night, as her fingers began their routine of moving from one bead to another, she discovered to her horror that all the beads were stuck together. Desperate, she began to cry.

Then she dried her tears and said, "It is now my turn to go and search for them."

She put on the younger brother's clothes, saddled her horse and, after riding for a long time, she came to the foot of the mountain where the little old man was.

When he saw her, the little old man began to laugh.

"You can't fool me! You are a woman and you will be even less able to climb the mountain than the others. Your brothers could not do it and neither will you."

"Yes, I will," she answered. "And I will find my brothers."

The old man shrugged and threw the marble.

"Wherever this little marble lands, you will get off your horse and start walking. And never look back, no matter what you hear. If you do not look back, you might be able to come to the place of the talking bird, the singing tree and the fountain of gold."

The girl began to climb. Behind her she heard horrible voices.

"We are going to put a knife through you!" And an icy cold wind blew behind her.

"Careful! There is a scorpion behind you!" And it seemed as if a thousand scorpions were running down her back.

"Look back! The hairy hand is catching up with you!" And she felt a stinking, hairy hand touching her neck.

They shouted. They whispered. They howled. But she kept climbing amidst stones of every size imaginable.

When she had almost reached the top of the mountain, she felt something damp and slimy touch her hair. She was about to look back when she suddenly heard wonderful music coming from the mountain peak just ahead. She took a deep breath and struggled to the top.

And there stood the talking bird with its feathers of fire, inside a golden cage.

"*Ecole cua*," it said when it saw her.

"What a funny bird," she thought to herself. "Is this all it can say?"

"*Ecole cua*," said the bird again. "Well done! Now you will recover not only your brothers, but that whole pile of stony people left behind on the way. Fill that jug with water from the fountain and pour a bit over each stone. You will see how they turn back into what they once were."

That is what the girl did. Moistened with the water from the fountain, the stones came back to life one by one. Finally, one of them turned into her older brother and a bit farther on she discovered the younger one. Both were surprised and delighted to see what their sister had accomplished.

Then the bird said, "Now we belong to you. Take a branch from the tree. And fill that jug with water from the fountain. As for me, take me with you just as I am."

The three siblings descended the mountain with their treasures. In their garden they planted the branch and the singing tree grew to full size. They emptied the jug and the fountain of gold began to flow. And the talking bird became their friend and advisor.

The two brothers were very good hunters. One afternoon they went to hunt wild boars. By chance they came into the same forest where the king was hunting.

Suddenly, out of the bush appeared a ferocious wild boar and it hurled itself on the king. The older brother who was pursuing it aimed his arrow and killed it.

"You have saved my life," the king said. "How can I repay you?"

The brothers answered that no compensation was necessary.

"Then at least accept an invitation to have lunch with me at the palace tomorrow," said the king.

Back at home the brothers told the bird what had happened. The bird nodded.

"That is fine. Go, but in turn, you will invite the king to come and have lunch with us."

So at the end of lunch, the young men invited the king to visit their house and their sister. The king accepted the invitation with pleasure. But when the sister heard about it she was worried.

"What shall I serve the king?" she asked.

"Do not worry," said the bird. "Dig a hole under the singing tree and there you will find a little trunk full of pearls. You will make little pearl cakes. The king has never eaten those."

They dug the hole and there was the little trunk. All three siblings made little cakes and everything else that the bird told them to do.

On the appointed day, the king appeared with his retinue. The table was set with a lace tablecloth and all the splendid things that the talking bird had unveiled.

"First you must take the king on a walk in the garden," the bird whispered into their ears.

And the king said, "What wonderful singing! What birds can sing so sweetly?"

"No, your majesty," the brothers said. "Those are not birds but a singing tree."

"It cannot be!" the king exclaimed. "There is no such thing."

So they sat under the tree and the king was stunned by the beauty of its song. It was the music of crystal and water and wind over the reeds.

Then they took him to the fountain of gold.

"And what kind of marvel is this?" the king asked.

"It is a magic fountain," they said. And they told him how they had found it and about the bravery of their younger sister, and the king was even more stunned.

The time came to sit down to eat. The king found it very odd that they should have a bird as a centerpiece. The bird was quiet.

The king thought to himself that the bird was very strange, but he merely said, "What beautiful plumage this bird has! I spend a great deal of time roaming the forest and have seen many things, but never a bird such as this."

The bird remained silent.

They served the meal and the king bit into one of the little cakes.

"But what is this?" he exclaimed in surprise.

"Pearl cakes, your majesty," the young woman said.

"I have never tried anything like this either! I never dreamed I could see what I am seeing today," said the king. "It is incredible!"

Then the bird spoke.

"It is not so incredible after all, your majesty."

The king's mouth fell open when he heard the bird speak, but the bird kept talking as calmly as ever.

"What I am going to tell you is even more unbelievable. It so happens that you are sitting at the table with your three children."

And while the king sat stupefied, the bird told him everything.

"...and the queen has nothing to do with what has happened and you have kept her in that cage all these years," concluded the bird. "So now that you know the truth, the time has come for you to take your children and the singing tree and the fountain of gold and me, and all of us shall go and live at the palace."

The king was speechless with emotion.

Finally he said, "Let us go right away because I

cannot even bear to think that I have kept an innocent woman, the wife I so loved, in a cage all these years." And he embraced everyone, especially his brave daughter.

The first thing they did when they got to the palace was to get the queen out of the cage. She laughed and cried at the same time when she heard what had happened to her children. Then they put the envious sisters in jail. And they lived very happily with the singing tree, the fountain of gold and the talking bird which, by the way, never stopped talking.

Ecole cua.

ABOUT THE AUTHORS

Pilar Almoina de Carrera was a professor of Spanish American literature and a scholar specializing in oral literature. For years she compiled and analyzed traditional and popular literature and published widely on the subject of folklore. She was a professor of post-graduate literary studies at the Universidad Central de Venezuela. She is the author of several books, including *Éste era una vez* (Caracas, Inciba, 1969), *El camino de Tío Conejo* (Caracas, Ministry of Education, 1970) and *Había una vez ventiséis cuentos* (Caracas, Ediciones Ekaré, 1985). She died suddenly in February, 2000.

Pascuala Corona is the pseudonym of Teresa Castelló de Yturbide, a compiler of Mexican tales from pre-Columbian times to the present. Her main sources have been nannies – the great storytellers – and among them her own whose name was Pascuala Corona. Teresa Castelló was born on the first day of spring which, according to her, means that "even if they cut you down many times, as with a tree, you sprout again, you begin to live again." She is the author of more than twenty-five books on Mexican art and tradition, including several children's books.

Rafael Olivares Figueroa was born in Caracas in 1893 and died in 1972. He was a poet, essayist, compiler and scholar of folklore. For many years he lived in Spain and was a founding member of the Frente Literario of Madrid. He returned to Venezuela in the thirties, became part of the avant-garde and with other noted scholars organized the National Folklore Institute. He collaborated on many periodicals and magazines in Venezuela and Spanish America. As a folklore expert he developed a body of work of enormous value, both in the reclaiming of materials and in their analysis.

Carmen Heny was born in Caracas, Venezuela, in the year of the great earthquake and died in 1997 at the age of ninety-seven. She spent her childhood on an hacienda where the peccary roamed during the day and night was a time for storytelling. She was descended from Alejandro Benítez, founder of Colonia Tovar, a town west of Caracas, where German settlers came to work in 1848. Many of her stories come from German folklore. These stories had been heard by her ancestors on European soil and told to their children and grandchildren. To these versions Carmen Heny added a native flavor of her own. She was one of Venezuela's pioneer women. She was a famous gardener, lover of flowers and of life, and one of the first women to drive a car in Caracas. She left a daughter, three grandchildren and ten adopted daughters. She is the co-author of *Tun, tun, quién es* (Caracas, Ediciones Ekaré, 1986).

Rafael Rivero Oramas is one of the outstanding figures of Venezuelan children's literature. He began to work in this field in 1926, when he founded three children's magazines: *El Fakir, Cuas Cuas* and *Caricatura*. In 1938 he founded the magazine *Onza, Tigre y León*, the best children's magazine the country has ever produced, and in 1949 the magazine *Tricolor*, which he edited until 1967. From 1931 to 1962 he directed and wrote a radio program called *Las Aventuras del Tío Nicolás*, in which he told stories and legends, and which made him famous all over Venezuela. In 1965 he published *La danta blanca*, the first Venezuelan adventure novel for children. In 1973 *El mundo de Tío Conejo* was published – one of the most outstanding collections of stories based on the character Tío Conejo.

Margot Silva Pérez was born in Barcelona at the turn of the century and died in Caracas in 1983. She was a sweet and generous woman who told children beautiful stories in a whisper. But Margot was also a brave woman, a pioneer in the feminist movement and a tenacious fighter for Venezuelan democracy. She marched to Guatire with the students jailed in 1928; she was detained by the Gómez government police in La Guaira while weighed down with propaganda against the dictator, she was exiled to Trinidad but returned after Gómez's death to participate in Organización Revolucionaria de Venezuela in 1936 and later in the Asociación Cultural Femenina, where she fought for the vote for Venezuela's women.

GLOSSARY

capybara: A large aquatic South American mammal. An excellent swimmer, it is the largest rodent in the world.

chitlings: The small intestine of swine, especially when prepared as food.

ecole cua: A popular saying meaning, "You've got it right!" or "That's it!"

hacienda: A large estate for farming or ranching or the main house on the estate.

machete: A heavy knife, much like a sword, used as a weapon or for cutting.

mamón: Genip, a tropical American tree or bush that bears a round, edible fruit.

mondongo stew: Stew made from animal intestines.

tolete: A rounded stick used to grind maize.

wattle: The fleshy lobe that hangs from the neck or head of certain birds such as the turkey.

yucca: A New World plant with stiff, sword-shaped leaves and clusters of white flowers.